Ziggy Marley

Music Is in Everything

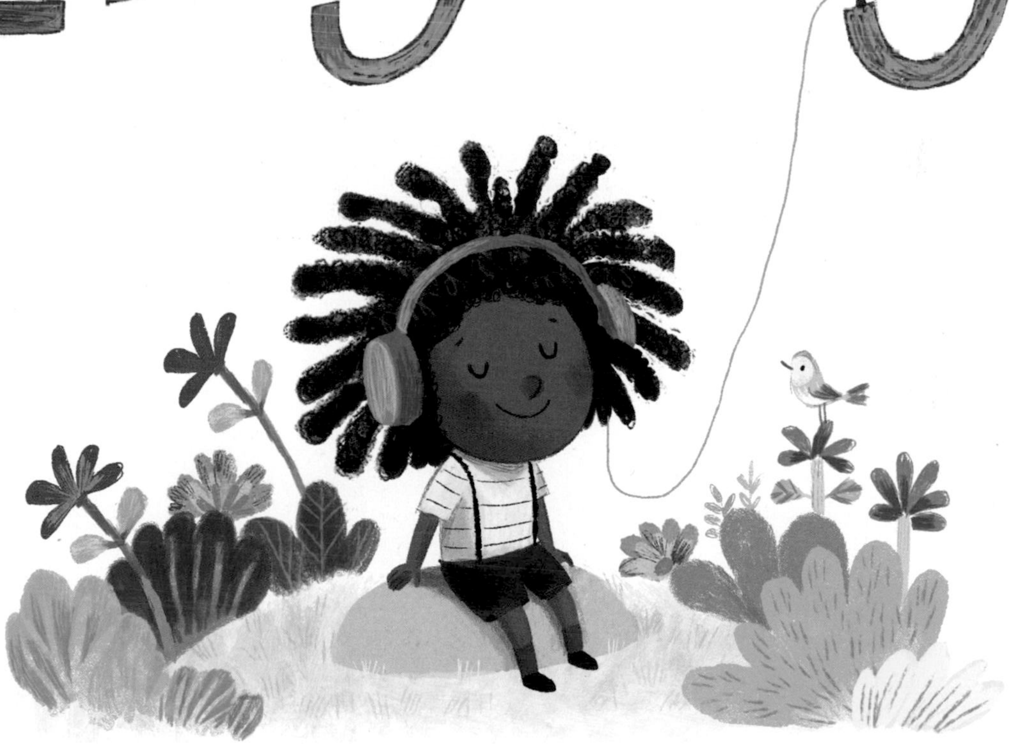

Music is in everything,

listen to the ocean sing.

Trees dance as the wind blows.

Pots and Pans

they make good sound!

Families now gather 'round,
there's a concert Saturday afternoon.

Join us in the kitchen
as we make our rhythm.

Grandma, Grandpa,
you'll be dancing, too.

Make a rice shaker,
let's eat dinner later.

Raindrops really locked into the groove.

Laughing

is a nice sound,

spreading joy all around.

Have you heard the river's latest tune?

Music is in everything,
listen to the birds they sing.

The bees dance as the honey flows.

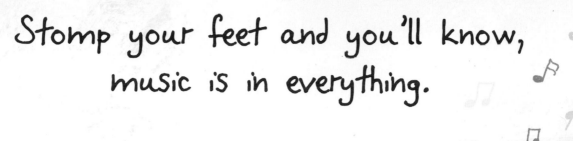

Stomp your feet and you'll know,
music is in everything.

Pots and pans they make good sound,
families now gather 'round,
there's a concert Saturday afternoon.

Join us in the kitchen
as we make our rhythm.

Uncle, Auntie, you'll be dancing, too.
Make a rice shaker,
let's eat dinner later.

really locked into the groove.

Laughing is a nice sound,
spreading joy all around.
Have you heard the river's lates

Music is in everything,
listen to the ocean sing.

MuSiC is in everything

Words by Ziggy Marley
Illustrations by Ag Jatkowska

Executive produced by Tuff Gong Worldwide

© 2022 Tuff Gong Worldwide, LLC
© 2020 "Music Is in Everything" lyrics published by Ishti Music, Inc.

Published by Akashic Books/Tuff Gong Worldwide Books
ISBN: 978-1-61775-943-7
Library of Congress Control Number: 2020948043

First printing
Printed in China

Akashic Books
Brooklyn, New York
Instagram/Twitter/Facebook:
AkashicBooks
E-mail: info@akashicbooks.com
Website: www.akashicbooks.com

ZIGGY MARLEY is an eight-time **GRAMMY** Award winner, Emmy Award winner, author, philanthropist, and reggae icon. He has released thirteen albums to much critical acclaim, and is the author of three other children's books: *I Love You Too*, *My Dog Romeo*, and *Little John Crow* (with his wife Orly Marley); as well the *Ziggy Marley and Family Cookbook*. His early immersion in music came at age ten when he sat in on recording sessions with his father, Bob Marley. Ziggy Marley and the Melody Makers released eight best-selling albums that garnered three **GRAMMY**s. Ziggy's second solo release, *Love Is My Religion*, won a **GRAMMY** in 2006 for Best Reggae Album. His third solo studio album, *Family Time*, scored a fifth **GRAMMY** award for Best Children's Album. 2016 marked the release of Marley's self-titled album, which earned his eighth **GRAMMY**. Marley's latest children's album, *More Family Time*, was released in 2020 via Tuff Gong Worldwide.

Also available from Ziggy Marley

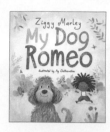

MY DOG ROMEO by Ziggy Marley • Illustrations by Ag Jatkowska
A children's picture book

Ziggy Marley's ode to his four-legged friend Romeo becomes a picture book that is sure to touch the hearts of dog lovers everywhere.

LITTLE JOHN CROW by Ziggy Marley and Orly Marley
Illustrations by Gordon Rowe
A children's picture book

After being abandoned by his animal friends, Little John Crow must come to terms with what it means to be part of a community when you are a vulture.

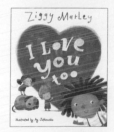

I LOVE YOU TOO by Ziggy Marley • Illustrations by Ag Jatkowska
A children's picture book

"A sweetly affectionate ode to togetherness and love." *—Publishers Weekly*

"Sure to be a hit at bedtime, the lyrical story conveys the sweet, soothing, and affirming message." *—School Library Journal*

ZIGGY MARLEY AND FAMILY COOKBOOK

"Ziggy's first collection of recipes pays homage to the flavors of his youth and the food he loves to cook for his wife and five children." *—People*

"With a health-focused approach, Ziggy Marley reveals memories and food traditions in his new family cookbook." *—Ebony*

How to make a shaker

Step 1.

Gather supplies
- Small pieces (rice, beans, jelly beans, small stones, or anything that will make noise)
- Container (water bottle, mason jar, thermos, etc.)
- Decorations (markers, paint, stickers, etc.—optional)
- Tape (optional)

Step 2.

Add your small pieces into container

- Fill container at least halfway
- Experiment to find the sound you like